MR DOG

AND A HEDGE CALLED HOG

BEN FOGLE

with Steve Cole

Illustrated by Ni

HarperCollins *Children's Books*

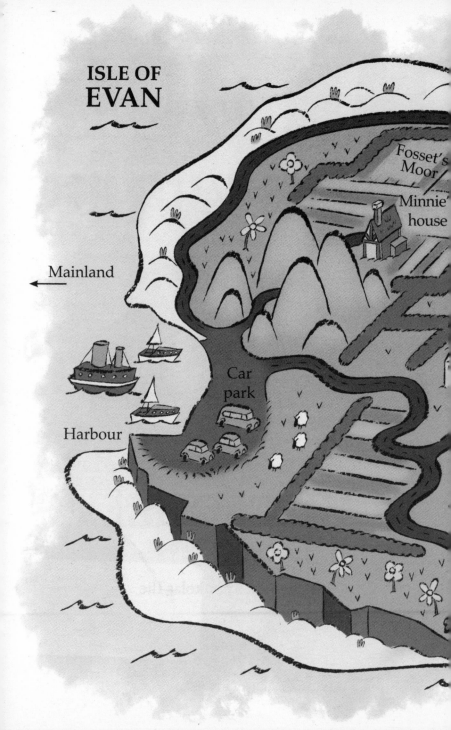

About the Author

BEN FOGLE is a broadcaster and seasoned adventurer. A modern-day nomad and journeyman, he has travelled to more than a hundred countries and accomplished amazing feats; from swimming with crocodiles to rowing three thousand miles across the Atlantic Ocean; from crossing Antarctica on foot to surviving a year as a castaway on a remote Hebridean island. Most recently, Ben climbed Mount Everest. Oh, and he LOVES dogs.

Books by Ben Fogle

MR DOG AND THE RABBIT HABIT

MR DOG AND THE SEAL DEAL

MR DOG AND A HEDGE CALLED HOG

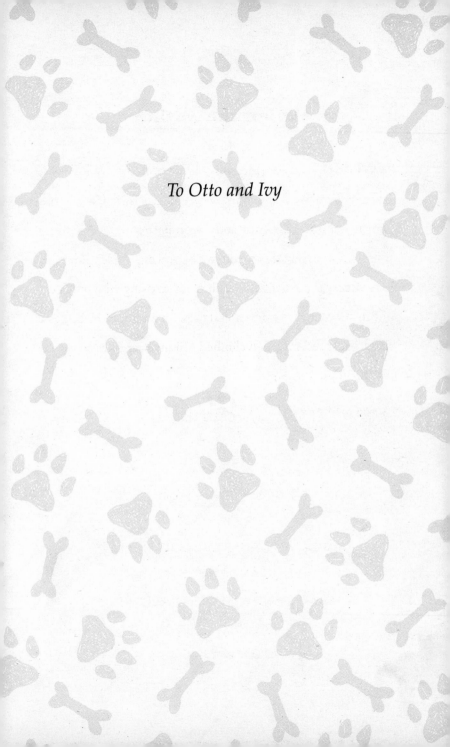

To Otto and Ivy

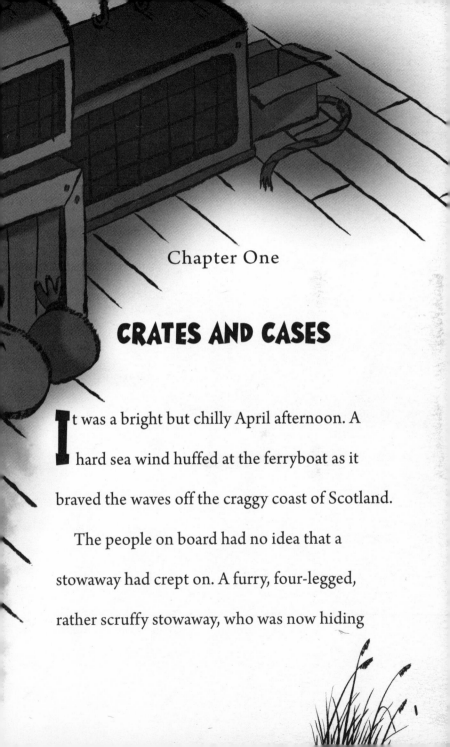

Chapter One

CRATES AND CASES

It was a bright but chilly April afternoon. A hard sea wind huffed at the ferryboat as it braved the waves off the craggy coast of Scotland.

The people on board had no idea that a stowaway had crept on. A furry, four-legged, rather scruffy stowaway, who was now hiding below deck in the cargo hold! Aside from his white beard and front paws, his fur was dark and shaggy. A ragged red-and-white hanky was tied about his neck. His ears were floppy, his nose was large and his brown eyes sparkled even in the gloom.

He wasn't just a dog. He was *Mr* Dog.

Mr Dog was a big fan of adventures, so he'd been roaming all over, from the south of England way up to the highlands of Scotland. It was there that he'd spied a group of people in a pretty little town catching the ferryboat to some islands off the coast, so he had crept into the cargo hold to go with them – and now, here he was!

To his surprise, he had found the hold mostly full of animal crates and carriers – at least forty of them. From the smell, he could tell that they had been used very recently. Some of them still had a few crushed dog biscuits inside (although with a hungry Mr Dog around, not for long). The funny thing, though, was that the crates didn't smell of dogs or cats or even of rabbits or rats, but of another animal – one that Mr Dog couldn't quite recognise. Someone had left a little fresh water in some of the bowls, so Mr Dog was glad of that.

Finally, the ferryboat slowed as it neared its destination, and Mr Dog felt the usual thrill of excitement at being about to explore somewhere new. 'Now, how to get off without being seen?' he mused.

Just then, the door to the hold was thrown open. Mr Dog ducked inside a pet carrier with solid plastic sides as a lady with frizzy blonde hair, wearing a bright red coat, bustled inside.

'I can see Jed's pick-up truck waiting,' the lady called to one of the crew. 'He'll help me unload the empty crates.'

'Right you are, Lizzie,' a woman called back.

How kind of this Jed to help Lizzie – and to help me too! thought Mr Dog. *I may as well stay in here and be carried off in style . . .*

Sure enough, once the boat had moored up, Jed came aboard and helped frizzy-haired Lizzie shift the crates and cages out of the hold. It took several trips. Mr Dog held his breath as his own carrier was lifted up.

'This one weighs a ton!' Jed declared.

How dare you! thought Mr Dog with a secret chuckle.

As soon as his carrier was put down, Mr Dog cautiously nosed open the door and peered out. He was in the back of Jed's pick-up truck, which was as red as Lizzie's coat and parked on a pier beside a small rocky harbour. Suddenly, he heard angry voices from beside a dark green van parked close by. Lizzie was arguing with another woman, whose sharp features reminded Mr Dog of a hunting bird, and he raised his ears to listen in.

'If I'd known you were only going over to the mainland to bring back more spotlights, Mrs Maitland, I'd have thrown them overboard!' said Lizzie hotly. 'What you've been doing to those hedgies is plain cruel!'

Mr Dog was puzzled. 'Cruelty to hedgies?' he murmured. 'Whatever does she mean?'

Mrs Maitland remained calm and haughty. 'They don't belong on the Isle of Evan, Lizzie. We'll get rid of them a lot faster by hunting them down than by taking them over to the mainland in crates . . .'

'Rubbish!' Lizzie insisted. 'Your hunts are dangerous and unnecessary and they're going to stop – mark my words.'

'Are they indeed!' Mrs Maitland sneered.

'Is a hedgie like a hedge?' Mr Dog wondered aloud (although to humans, of course, it came out as *Grrr, wuff-wuff RUFF!*). He jumped down from Jed's pick-up truck and trotted past the other side of Mrs Maitland's green van, shaking his head. 'I should think it *is* unnecessary to hunt down a hedge – it just stands there and lets you find it!'

'They're not talking about hedges.' A large, sturdy tan basset hound in a thick leather collar leaned through the van window. 'They're talking about *hedgehogs*.'

'Hedgehogs!' Mr Dog grinned. 'Of course, *that* was the smell in those cages. Wait a moment. *Why* are hedgehogs being taken to the mainland? Why don't they belong on this island?'

'Who cares?' said the basset hound. 'If

Mrs Maitland says they don't, then they don't.

She's my mistress, after all.'

'So Mrs Maitland is hunting these *hedgies*?'

'No, dogs like me are hunting them.' The basset hound looked confused. 'Aren't you hunting them too?'

'Goodness, no! The only things I'm hunting are happy memories.' He raised a paw. 'I'm Mr Dog, by the way.'

'My name's Dandy.' The basset hound looked suspiciously at Mr Dog. 'I've never seen you before on the island. Did you come over from the mainland with Lizzie? Or "Lizzie Toddy, busybody", as my mistress calls her.'

Mr Dog was not impressed by name-calling. 'I did come over from the mainland,' he said, 'but not with Lizzie. I just cadged a lift in the boat.'

'Well, perhaps you'd like to join us on the hunt tonight?' said Dandy. 'It's a good chase with all the other sniffer dogs, plus it's even more fun in the dark.'

'So *that's* why you need the spotlights! Hedgehogs only come out at night.' Mr Dog sighed. He always felt sorry for an underdog – or an under*hog* in this case. 'Well, thanks for the invite to the hunt, but no thanks. I hope it all goes wonderfully well . . .' As he turned, he added quietly, 'for the hedgehogs!'

'I heard that!' Dandy's hackles rose. 'Well, just make sure you stay out of the way of my hunting pals and me . . . and don't make friends with any hedgies if you know what's good for you.'

'Perhaps I should change my name to Mr *Doog*?' Mr Dog grinned. 'Then I'd know what's *good* for me backwards!'

By now, Mrs Maitland had loaded her spotlights into her van and was clambering into the driver's seat beside Dandy. 'Stop grumbling, boy!' she snapped at his low growls. 'I'm the one who should grumble, having to deal with Lizzie Toddy, busybody . . .'

Dandy barked an '*I told you so*' at Mr Dog. Then the van's engine started and Mr Dog scampered away. Mrs Maitland and Dandy drove off, then Lizzie and Jed drove away in the opposite direction.

Mr Dog trotted up the nearest grassy hillside to take a good look around at his surroundings and plan his next steps. But, really, he already knew what he was going to do.

'It sounds like the Isle of Evan's hedgies could use a good friend,' he declared. 'Luckily, good friends don't come any shaggier or waggier than Mr Dog!'

Chapter Two

A HEDGE CALLED HOG

As the sun sank lower in the sky, Mr Dog made his way through sloping meadows that were carpeted with long grass and rich with flowers.

Wind-blown trees pointed inland, to where the fields were spread out like patchwork with thick hedges at their edges.

'But are there any hedg*ies* in the hedges?' Mr Dog wondered aloud as he trotted onward. He wanted to warn as many of the little animals as he could about the hunt. It was a large island, though, and he didn't even know where the hunt would be taking place.

Still, I have to try, he thought.

Once Mr Dog reached the first hedge, he pushed his nose underneath. He sniffed all the way along to the next field but couldn't find any hedgehogs.

He caught a sniff of the little snufflers in the spiky hedgerow in the next field, but again he couldn't work out their location. Sleeping by day,

they were well hidden and safe from sight – but

not from the sniffer dogs trained to hunt them

down in the darkness.

As Mr Dog was wondering what to do, he

spotted a hare hopping through the waving grass.

'I say!' he called. 'Could I ask you for directions?'

'To where?' wondered the hare.

'To the nearest

hedgehogs!' Mr Dog said

with a grin.

The hare looked

wary. 'Ah. You must

be one of those

hunting hounds.'

'Must I?' Mr Dog frowned. 'Why? Have you seen some hunting hounds out lately?'

'I have, yes. Out on Fosset's Moor,' the hare went on. 'I was chased by a ridgeback and a bloodhound there this morning. They told me they'd catch me if I was back again tonight. Well, not likely!'

'That's interesting.' Mr Dog wagged his tail thoughtfully. 'It sounds as if the hunt will be on Fosset's Moor.' He barked across to the hare. 'If you tell me where Fosset's Moor is, I'll tell those hounds to leave you alone!'

'Oh. Thanks, friend.' The hare thumped his back leg. 'Keep travelling east in a straight line.

Once you've climbed the hill, you'll be looking down over Fosset's Moor.'

'I'm *moor* than grateful to you!'

With a woof of farewell, Mr Dog scampered away. He ran through fields of heather, vaulted over fences, jumped over a ditch, doubled back to drink some water from the ditch, then on he ran again.

Half an hour later, as it was starting to get dark, he reached the steep hillside that the hare had described. Trotting to the top, he found a large stretch of grassland sloping away from him, lined with long, tangled rows of bushes.

'Time to investigate,' he panted, and sniffed

his way along the old, gnarled hedgerow. Many scents caught in his nostrils – honeysuckle, harvest mice, hawthorn . . . and HEDGEHOG! *Yes*, thought Mr Dog with growing excitement. It was the same smell he'd noticed in Lizzie Toddy's crates. And with night falling, the hedgies would be waking up.

Mr Dog searched about more carefully. He found a pile of damp leaves and twigs, but the long grass tickled his nose and made him sneeze.

'EEK!' the leaves seemed to squeal and Mr

Dog jumped back in surprise.

'Hello?' He got down on his belly and crawled

a little closer. 'Anyone there?'

'No,' came a quivering voice.

'Oh.' Mr Dog frowned and cocked his head.

'Are you sure no one's there?'

'ACHOO!'

'Definitely not!' said the shaky voice. 'No hedgehogs here. Only a hedge.'

Mr Dog couldn't help but smile. 'So, I'm talking to a hedge?'

'Yes, you are, and the hedge isn't talking back to you,' the voice said. 'So there.'

'Is that so?' Mr Dog replied. 'Well, thank you for letting me know.'

'You're welcome.'

'I'm welcome? In that case, I'll come back!' Mr Dog eagerly pushed his head back under the bushes. 'Hello!'

'EEK!' came the squeal again.

'There's no need to be afraid,' said Mr Dog.

'Tell me, does this hedge have a name?'

'Hog,' came the little voice.

'A hedge called Hog, eh?' Mr Dog grinned. 'You know, I think it's more likely you're a hog called Hedge!'

'No! My name *is* Hog, honest . . .' In the twilight, Mr Dog saw a little black nose push out from the leaves. Two beady black eyes and a spiky fringe followed close behind. Before he knew it, Mr Dog was snout to snout with a young hedgehog!

'EEP!' Hog's eyes widened with alarm and, in a heartbeat, he rolled himself up into a spiky ball.

Mr Dog blinked. 'Goodness, I wish I could

do a trick like that. Although then I suppose I'd

have to call myself Mr *Hog* instead of Mr Dog.'

'Whoever you are, you're scary,' said

Hog, trembling.

'*Hairy*, yes. Scary, never,' said Mr Dog. 'The D-O-G in my name stands for Delightful Old Gentleman! Well, probably.'

'My mum told me about dogs!' Hog's quills quivered as he spoke. 'She told me that the two-legged giants take sniffy dogs and go hunting for hedgies.'

'I think you mean "sniffer" dogs,' said Mr Dog.

'The sniffing sniffy sniffer dogs sniff us out, and the giants sweep sticks through the long grass and poke us hedgies into the open.' Hog gave a long, snuffling sigh. 'And we're never seen again.'

'What a terrible story! Wait.' Mr Dog reversed

out from under the hedgerow and sniffed the air. 'I can smell something . . .'

'Maybe it's an escaping hedgehog!' Hog squealed and beetled away along the side of the hedgerow, heading down the hillside. 'Goodbye, scary dog! I'm off!'

'Hog, come back!' It had grown dark, but Mr Dog's senses were keen. His nose was filling with wet, animal smells. At the same time, he saw bright lights bobbing up the hill towards him, the same way he'd come. There were noises too: a thumping, crashing sound and excited yelps. Hounds – and lots of them.

'Good boy, Dandy!' Mrs Maitland's voice

carried through the darkness. 'Have you found one? Found a hedgehog for us . . . ?'

'Oh, dear!' Mr Dog ran down the hill after the little hedgehog as the crashing got closer. 'The hunt is coming, Hog – and I'm afraid they're hunting you!'

Chapter Three

A FIGHT IN THE NIGHT!

Mr Dog soon caught up with Hog, who was beetling towards the nearest hedgerow. 'You led the hunt to me!' he squealed, prickles rippling over his body as he ran. 'You're a big, mean sniffy dog!'

'I did not lead anyone to you,' Mr Dog

insisted. 'And if those hounds find us, you'll have the proof. Now, keep running!'

'I can't!' Hog puffed. 'I have to hide!'

'They will sniff you out,' Mr Dog told him. 'We have to outrun them.'

It sounded as if the scrum of people and hounds was crashing ever closer to the top of the hill. The lights blazed into view like an approaching fire, turning the dark fields floodlit, and the yips and barks of the dogs rose in pitch.

'Dandy, no!' Mrs Maitland shouted crossly. 'Come back here!'

Mr Dog gasped as a familiar figure jumped into sight over the hill. Dandy the basset hound

had escaped his owner to pursue the hedgehog alone, his lead trailing behind him.

'Faster! Faster! Must run faster!' Hog repeated the words over and over, his little paws tearing across the turf.

Mr Dog knew that the hedgehog was just too slow.

Dandy only had little legs himself, but he was closing fast. 'Curl up, Hog, quickly!'

With a desperate squeal, Hog tucked himself into a ball. Mr Dog turned and reared up on his back legs to block the basset hound, but Dandy dodged him and then – BAM! – swiped at Hog with the side of his head. In so doing, Dandy got a cheekful of prickles and yelped.

Mr Dog saw poor Hog bounce and bump away down the hillside like a football. Angrily,

he pushed his head under Dandy's low-hanging stomach and flipped the hound over, barking as scarily as he could. Caught off-guard, his cheek still stinging, Dandy backed away. The baying hounds were very close now, straining forward with their handlers. Mrs Maitland led the charge, grabbing Dandy's lead before he could escape again.

'A dog helping a hedgehog instead of his own kind?' Dandy snarled. 'You'll regret this, scruff-bag. My pals and I will get you, just you wait!'

'Sorry, no time to wait!' Mr Dog bounded away after Hog. 'I've a talking hedge to look out for!'

Hog had tumbled down to the bottom of

the hill and was lying on his back with his eyes closed, panting for breath. He looked to be in a total daze.

Mr Dog cast a nervous look back at the pack of dogs hurrying down the hill towards them. Each bark was like a blade slicing through the night. 'There's no time to lose,' he murmured. Carefully, Mr Dog closed his jaws round Hog, lifted him up and ran away. He ducked through a hedgerow and sped across a fallow field, putting as much distance as he could between himself and the hunting party. *On the lead, those dogs can only move as fast as their handlers,* he thought. *They shouldn't be too hard to outrun!*

But Mr Dog could hear the warning in the

howls the pack threw after him: *'We won't always*

be on the lead. Just you wait, scruff-bag – we're

going to get you and that hog . . . and there'll be no

humans to stop us!'

Mr Dog carried Hog delicately between his

teeth for what had to be more than a mile before finally he stopped on high ground further round the coast. His jaws were aching and his tongue was sore from prickles. Trying not to pant, he listened hard but could hear only the roar of the sea below, crashing on rocks

somewhere in the darkness beneath.

The stars were bright and the moon was up now, and full. Mr Dog padded over to a hunched-over tree and gently placed Hog beneath it on a bed of leaves. As far as he could tell, the little hedgie was uninjured. To keep Hog safe, he covered him over with more leaves and then lay down beside him, exhausted.

Soon Mr Dog fell into an uneasy sleep, ears twitching for any sound of the hounds. He was fond himself of hunting about after interesting smells, and knew that some hounds – particularly in more remote places – were bred to do nothing else. However, he knew that a few liked to hunt

so much that they got overexcited, determined to catch their prey whatever it took. That made them dangerous to anyone who got in their way.

He jumped at the sound of movement beside him, but it was only Hog wriggling into sight through the leaves.

'Oh, what horrible dreams I've had,' squealed the hedgehog. He sniffed and stared about. 'Where are my friends? Where am I?'

'I wish I knew,' said Mr Dog. 'I'm a stranger here myself.'

'Aaaagh!' Hog squealed like a little siren going off. 'It's you! I remember. You tried to eat me!'

'I only picked you up so I could carry you to

safety!' Mr Dog let his tongue dangle from his mouth. 'I got prickled by a prickle too.'

But the little hedgie was in another panic. 'I won't let you bite me!' His tiny legs propelled him out of the leaves and he scurried up the grassy slope towards a rocky ledge. 'I'm off!'

'Hog, wait,' Mr Dog yelped. 'It's not safe!'

The panicking hedgehog was running straight for the edge of a cliff!

Chapter Four

HELPING HOG

Mr Dog raced after him and barked, 'STOP!'

Such was the power in that ear-shaking

woof that the hedgehog jumped, skidded and

spun round. He found himself on one paw,

teetering on the edge of a long drop down to the

rocky shoreline far below.

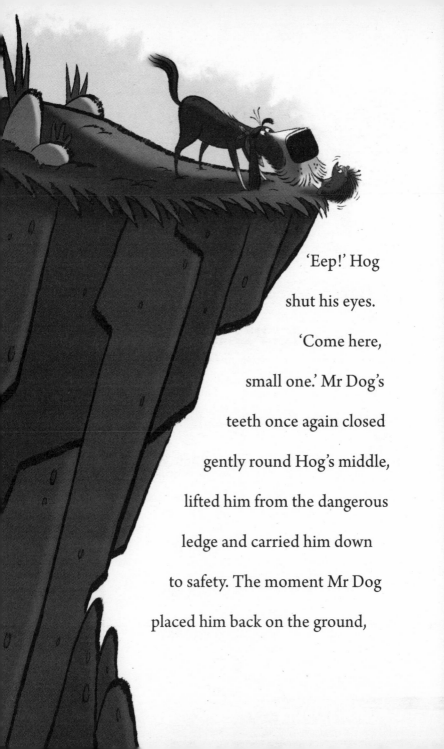

'Eep!' Hog
shut his eyes.
'Come here,
small one.' Mr Dog's
teeth once again closed
gently round Hog's middle,
lifted him from the dangerous
ledge and carried him down
to safety. The moment Mr Dog
placed him back on the ground,

Hog tucked himself back into a trembling ball.

'We're close to the cliffs, you silly spiky thing,' Mr Dog scolded. 'You really must trust me. I'm a friend to all animals.'

'All right.' Hog poked out his nose and opened one eye. 'I'm sorry if I was rude. But you sniffy dogs are very scary to a little hedge like me. Not just your teeth. Those dirty great paws of yours could squash me flat.'

'Dirty paws? How dare you! I'm extremely clean.' Mr Dog wiped his front paws in the dew and kicked up some grass with the back ones. 'See? I promise not to squash you, Hog. I just want to get you to safety. Now where do you live – under that hedgerow?'

'Nope. I don't really have a home.' Small tears welled up in Hog's beady black eyes. 'I usually just wander about, sometimes with my friends. But that was until something awful happened . . .'

Mr Dog lay down beside him. 'Tell me about it.'

'I was out with some friends, looking for food,' Hog went on, unfolding himself as he talked. 'Sprackle said that he knew a field full of caterpillars, and Tucker thought we might even find some wader eggs.'

'From wader birds?' Mr Dog was surprised. 'You eat eggs?'

'Well, not me personally,' Hog admitted. 'But Sprackle and Tucker think they're the most delicious food ever. We thought that hunting for some would be a good adventure.' He snuffled quietly. 'But fog blew in from the sea and I lost my way. I couldn't find Sprackle and Tucker. Then I heard them cry out for help . . .' Hog quivered so much he almost curled up again. 'I looked for them, but couldn't see them anywhere. When the sun came up, I hid under that hedgerow and slept.'

Mr Dog nodded sympathetically. 'What about your family? Where are they?'

'I've no idea,' said Hog. 'A hoglet leaves his

family behind when he's five or six weeks, and I'm nearly four seasons old now.'

'Well, Hog, they do say that travel broadens the mind, and I'm sure it sharpens the prickles too.' Mr Dog wagged his shaggy broom of a tail.

'I'm here to help you. Perhaps we can find—'

Hog sprang up in the air. 'A BEETLE.'

Mr Dog was confused. 'Well, I suppose we *could* find a beetle, but I actually meant—'

'No, I mean, I just heard a beetle.' Hog was already snuffling away through the grass, licking his lips. 'Mmmm, come to me, beetle . . . OM, NOM, NOM!' He munched the insect down. 'It may not be a wader egg . . . but it's delicious!'

Mr Dog smiled down at the scatty little hedgie. He wondered what on earth cute animals like this had done to get Mrs Maitland cross enough to send out hunting parties. *'They don't belong on the Isle of Evan,'* she'd said – but WHY didn't they?

'As I was saying,' Mr Dog went on, 'perhaps we could find a lady called Lizzie Toddy who lives on this island. She came over on the same boat as me and she seemed to like hedgehogs.'

'What's a boat?' Hog asked.

'It's a thing humans use to travel over water,' Mr Dog explained. 'Lizzie had all sorts of crates and cases for carrying hedgehogs, and wanted to stop the hunt. Perhaps if we find her, she will help you.'

Hog looked up at Mr Dog, his black eyes wide and bright. 'Do you really think she would?'

'I think it's worth a try.' Mr Dog sighed. 'Unfortunately, I have no idea where she is or how we can find her.' He brightened, licking his chops. 'Still, the island can't be that big, can it? And she was in a big red pick-up, so she must live near a road . . .'

'Roads are a bit scary,' said Hog. 'They have big metal things on them that roar and try to squish you.'

'We'll take extra care,' Mr Dog assured him. Then he held up a paw for quiet. Distantly, blown on the wind, he could hear the bark and yap of excited hounds. 'Uh-oh. Sounds like the pack is back.'

'EEEEP!' Hog had already rolled himself up into a ball.

Mr Dog smiled down at the little hedgehog. 'We'd better get moving.'

Hog pushed out his nose. 'But where to?' he twittered.

'Perhaps down to the beach.' Mr Dog walked carefully back to the ledge of the cliff and surveyed the steep descent. 'A dog can manage a tough climb, but the hounds' human handlers won't want to chance it. They'll hopefully give up and leave us be—'

'Leave us BEETLE?' said Hog excitedly.

Mr Dog frowned. 'No. Just leave us be.'

'Oh.' Hog stuck out his tongue. 'Bees don't taste very nice. I much prefer beetles.'

'Escape first,' said Mr Dog, 'beetles later.' He paused. 'Do you think you could try not to curl up while I carry you? My tongue could use a rest from prickles.'

Hog shifted uncomfortably but nodded. Mr Dog delicately picked him up in his jaws and set off, taking a careful path down the steep, muddy hillside. The dark sea frothed and hissed as it slapped against the strip of stony beach that huddled between this cliff face and the next. Surely the hunters couldn't possibly follow their hedgehog trail down here!

Mr Dog was just congratulating himself on his cleverness when a tuft of turf gave way beneath him.

He scrabbled at the wet mud and rock but

couldn't get a paw-hold, and started sliding down

the steep slope towards the sea!

'What's happening?' squeaked Hog.

'Hold on!' Mr Dog groaned through a

mouthful of prickles, paws still scrabbling at

stone and grass as he picked up speed. 'Looks

like we're taking the quick way down!'

Chapter Five

EGG-STRA SPECIAL

Mr Dog gave a howl of fear as he slid faster down towards the stony beach. Suddenly, he hit a grassy outcrop that sent him tumbling head-over-paws. To his horror, Hog had slipped from his mouth! The little hedgehog was bouncing off a boulder and flying up into the air. Mr Dog spread out his legs beneath the airborne hedgehog and flattened himself down on the ground to catch him. He gave a sigh of relief as the hedgie landed on his back!

'EEEEP!' Hog's little teeth chomped into Mr Dog's necktie and he clung on for dear life.

A jagged rock sticking out from the cliff face loomed in front of Mr Dog. Desperately, he pushed off from the rock with his paws to avoid hitting it full-on . . .

For a few moments, all he could feel was cold air ruffling through his fur, nothingness beneath his paws, and then . . .

Mr Dog and Hog plunged into freezing water.

Everything was black, and all noise was muffled.

Doggy-paddling furiously, he broke the surface

of the water. The sea roared in his ears and the air

was filled with salty spray.

'Hog?' barked Mr Dog. 'Where are you?'

'Right here!' came the little squeak of a voice

in his ear. Hog was still clinging on with paws and

jaws to Mr Dog, shaking with fright. 'What is this

giant, angry, salty puddle?'

'It's the sea,' Mr Dog spluttered, striking out

for shore. 'It's all around the island.'

'The sea? I see. Mr Dog, are you my boat?'

'That's right, Hog! Just hold on tight and we'll

be back on dry land in two shakes of a soggy tail!'

Swimming with all his might, Mr Dog reached the pebbly shore and dragged himself onto it. His body felt bruised and sore, and his tummy was red with scratches from the long slide down. Hog clambered over Mr Dog's head on to the wet beach. Then he waddled round and squeezed up against him, shivering with the cold. Mr Dog put a protective paw over him, his pads shielding him from the prickles.

They lay like that for a few minutes, then Mr Dog got up and led them to shelter at the base of the cliffs. High above, he could hear the yips and yaps of the hounds, and saw the blazing beams of the humans' hand-held searchlights.

'I don't suggest you follow us down here!' Mr Dog muttered.

After a few minutes, the searchlights faded and the barking died away. The hunters had moved away from the ledge.

'What do we do now?' asked Hog through tiny chattering teeth.

Mr Dog considered. It was an impossible climb back up. 'I think we had better try to walk round the shoreline for a while. It'll keep us out of the way of those hounds at least!'

Luckily, the tide was going out, so by splashing through the rockpools at the edge of the little cove, carrying Hog between his teeth, Mr Dog was able to reach the neighbouring beach. Mr Dog walked across the lonely stretch of sand, the sea hurling spray as it surged in and then hissed back out. He stopped for a brief rest, and looked at the craggy solitude around him. The sky was lightening, and seabirds wheeled and called from the cliffs as they woke and began their days.

Hog yawned. 'I should be asleep,' he said.

'That's why we have to keep moving now,' Mr Dog explained. 'The hounds won't be looking for you in daylight. It gives us more time to find Lizzie.'

But Hog wasn't listening. He had fallen asleep

on the sand, snuffling and snoring. With a smile, Mr Dog gently picked up the little hedgie with his teeth and, with some difficulty, tucked him inside his red-and-white neckerchief. Then he set off again.

The day warmed up as Mr Dog made his way round the coast, his tiny rider puffing in his ear with each snoozing breath. Eventually, the cliffs gave way to lower-lying dunes lined with sea kelp. A beautiful scent teased Mr Dog's nose, and as he climbed to the top of the dunes he found a spectacular carpet of wild flowers of all different colours: vivid reds, cheery yellows and bold purples. Sand flies spun in a haze above the

flowers, and the sweet-smelling grass seemed

alive with insects. That perhaps explained the

sheer number of wader birds gliding and striding

about – Mr Dog spotted dunlins and plovers and

coots and many more he didn't recognise. The air
was filled with trills and tweets and piping calls
of strange and unusual breeds.

Then he spotted some wooden shelters set
up further inland with slits in the walls. *Hides*,
thought Mr Dog. *Human bird-watchers must
use the hides to watch the birds here without
disturbing them. I suppose there must be* rare
birds around here.

Thirsty and hungry from all his exertions, Mr Dog lapped some dew from the grass beside a small mound. A bird with a bright red neck burst out from behind it with a sharp, screeching cry, and Mr Dog jumped. Then he noticed a small, untidy nest in the flowery grass. Four splotchy olive eggs sat inside it.

Hog started to wriggle in the grip of his raggedy collar. 'Ooooh! What's that whiff in my nose?' The little hedgie pulled himself free and dropped down to the fragrant turf. 'Oooooh, something smells delicious.'

Mr Dog frowned. 'The eggs, you mean?'

'EGGS!' Hog wiggled towards the eggs with

startling speed. 'At last. My friends said wader eggs were the best. Now I can taste them for myself!'

'Hog, wait!' Mr Dog stuck his nose right up to the hedgehog and nudged him aside. 'You shouldn't eat that egg. There's a little chick growing inside it!'

Hog tried to push past Mr Dog, his mouth watering. 'Pardon?'

'Well, would you like it if a bird ate a little baby hoglet?' Mr Dog demanded. 'Eat a bug or a beetle instead. They lay many more eggs at a time.'

'But hedgehogs are *always* eating bird eggs,' Hog protested. 'They're this island's top tasty

treat! We've been eating them for ages.'

Mr Dog gasped. 'Hog . . . perhaps that's it!'

'That's what?' said Hog, puzzled.

'The reason you hedgies are being hunted,'

said Mr Dog gravely. 'I think I've worked it out!'

Chapter Six

DANGER IN THE FIELDS

'**Y**ou told me that you hedgehogs keep eating wader eggs,' Mr Dog reminded Hog. 'Well, I'm a well-travelled animal and I don't recognise a lot of the birds here. I think there must be many rare breeds – which means they only lay their eggs in a very few places . . .'

'Oh. Oh, dear. I see what you're saying.' Hog looked up at Mr Dog, wide-eyed and prickles pointing. 'If hedgehogs eat all those eggs, there'll be no more new chicks hatching.'

'And the rare birds get even rarer,' Mr Dog agreed. 'The humans could be trying to protect them.'

'By getting rid of hedgies?' said Hog sadly. 'But we're only following our instincts. How could we know that some of these eggs are special?'

'I know,' said Mr Dog. 'And I still don't understand what Mrs Maitland meant when she said you hedgehogs didn't belong here.'

'It makes me want to hide away forever.' Hog looked up at Mr Dog. 'Perhaps I could pretend

to be a hedge again? I know I didn't fool you, but then you are *extra* clever.'

'True.' Mr Dog grinned. 'But I don't think anyone will believe you're a hedge. Now, come on. We have to try and find Lizzie Toddy "Busybody", and hope she's not *too* busy to help you and your friends!'

Mr Dog let Hog fill up on insects and caterpillars, and even munched on a couple of crickets himself. Then he carried the little hedgehog away through the thick carpet of flowers. A stream cut through the moorland, sloping sandy banks on each side. At last Mr Dog could drink and bathe the sore spots on his tongue from all of Hog's prickles.

They travelled along the hedgerows, so Hog

could warn any hedgies hiding there to watch

out for dogs, and Mr Dog could demonstrate

what a dog actually looked like. By the middle of

the afternoon, Hog had snuffled out the hiding

places of twenty-seven hedgehogs and had had a

quiet word with each, telling them to keep close

to cover, avoid eggs and pass on the information

to other hedgehogs.

'One last thing,' Hog said solemnly at the end

of every warning. 'Don't pretend to be a talking

hedge – it doesn't seem to work!'

As they walked through the fields, Mr Dog

kept his ear cocked for sounds of traffic, but there

were none.

'The nearest road could be miles away,'

Mr Dog muttered.

'Why are roads so important?' asked Hog,

looking up at him.

'They lead to farms and houses. I might pick

up Lizzie's scent on a road – or even spot her pick-up truck out and about. After all, this is only a small island.'

He spoke with as much confidence as he could, trying to reassure the little hedgehog. But really he knew they might wander the island together, lost, for days and nights. In the meantime, for all the hedgehogs they were warning, many more would be hunted by hounds and be at Mrs Maitland's mercy.

They stopped for a rest in a grassy field in which small sheep with black faces and brown tufty coats were grazing. The nearest ewes backed away at the sight of Mr Dog. One of them, braver than the rest, stamped a hoof.

'I'm too tired to chase you,' Mr Dog assured her.

'Hey, are you thirsty?' Hog was peering across the field and sniffing the air. 'I think there's a stream around here.'

'There is.' With his keener eyesight, Mr Dog could see the stream, cutting through the bottom of the field. Then he heard something – a low chugging and popping noise. It sounded like an engine!

'Get into a ball, Hog,' Mr Dog instructed. 'An engine means a vehicle – and that means a road. We need to see where it's coming from.'

The hedgehog curled up and rolled neatly into Mr Dog's jaws. 'I'm good to go!'

Mr Dog picked up Hog and hared away in search of the vehicle. He sent sheep scattering as he galloped past, and mumbled apologies.

The noise of the engine grew louder. At the bottom of the field stood an open gate, and Mr Dog saw an old, muddy tractor rumbling into view on enormous wheels.

'We'll take the direction it came from,' he decided, and changed course towards the tractor. But then the tractor stopped and its driver dropped down from inside, looking very angry!

'Chase my flock, would you?' The farmer, tall, lean and red-faced, pointed at Mr Dog, who skidded to a stop. 'You must be the wild mutt who was fighting Mrs Maitland's Dandy. Well, we don't stand for strays or sheep-worriers on the Isle of Evan!'

'I'm not wild – I'm really quite reasonable,'

Mr Dog protested. 'And your sheep aren't worried, they're just a little surprised!' But of course, his words came out just as woofs and wuffs to the farmer, and all muffled by a mouthful of hedgie. To Mr Dog's horror, the farmer reached inside the tractor's cab – and pulled out a shotgun.

'Goodbye!' Mr Dog turned tail and ran as fast as he could in the opposite direction, heading for the stream. BOOM! The shotgun fired. Mr Dog's eyes widened but he kept on running.

'EEEEP! What was that?' cried Hog.

'Nothing nice!' Mr Dog told him. Heart hammering, he put on a last desperate burst of speed. BOOM! The farmer fired again.

Sand sprayed from the bank just in front of Mr Dog and showered over him. Some went in his eyes. Blinded for a moment, he leaped for cover, tumbled down the bank and hit the stream.

The splash-landing knocked Hog from out of Mr Dog's jaws! With an 'EEEEEEP!' and a PLOP, the hedgehog hit the cold blue water . . . and sank from sight!

'Hog?' Mr Dog pushed his face into the water and blinked, trying to clear his eyes. 'Oh, Hog! What have I done?' He searched about more desperately. 'That poor prickled pickle – I've lost him in the water. He'll be drowned!'

Chapter Seven

ON THE ROAD

Mr Dog grew desperate, splashing about in a circle, looking for Hog. The farmer's voice carried across the field and over the bank, 'What's all that splashing? Did I hit him . . . ?'

Not yet, you didn't, thought Mr Dog. *And I'm*

not going to give you another chance! He knew he

had to leave. 'Oh, Hog . . .'

'Quickly, Mr Dog,' came a high, twittery voice

from the hedgerow on the far side of the stream.

'We must go!'

'What?' Mr Dog shook water from his ears.

'Who said that?'

'Well, it's not the hedge,

is it?' A familiar little

face with eyes as

black as his nose

pushed out from

the greenery.

'Hog!' Mr Dog

leaped from the water and gave his little friend a fond lick on the side of the face – before yelping at the sting of prickles. 'How did you get out of the water?'

Hog blinked. 'Didn't you know hedgehogs could swim?'

'No!' exclaimed Mr Dog.

'Well, neither did I,' Hog admitted. 'But we can! So I did. I swam right between your back legs and then crawled out to the hedgerow. I called to you but you were too busy splashing about. Now, come on!'

Mr Dog turned back to the field and stood up on his legs to see over the bank. The farmer was striding towards the stream with his gun. 'You're quite right, Hog. We must go at once.' He dug furiously at the sandy turf with his paws, trying to make a space big enough to fit through.

Hog tried to help, but was soon buried in a pile of sand! He pulled himself free and beetled through to the other side of the hedge. 'Oooh! Mr Dog, I spy a winding grey thing. I think it's a road.'

'Really?' Mr Dog squeezed and squashed through his little trench beneath the hedgerow and joined Hog on the other side. A narrow, single-track road full of bumps and potholes stretched alongside the farmer's field. 'You're right, Hog, it IS a road – and we'd better take it!'

Mr Dog grabbed Hog and tossed him in the air. Hog rolled up into a ball and Mr Dog made a perfect catch with his jaws – then took off at high speed. **BOOM!** Thunder burst from the farmer's shotgun one more time, but Mr Dog kept running until he was safely out of sight round the corner. Then he paused, panting for breath as he placed Hog back on the ground.

'Was that human trying to hurt you?' asked the hedgehog.

'I'm afraid so. He must've been on the hunt last night – he saw me fight off Dandy the basset, and now he thinks I'm a menace to other

80

animals, like his sheep.' Mr Dog sighed. 'Farmers have to guard their flocks well in isolated spots, as help is so hard to come by.'

'So is help for hedgehogs,' said Hog sadly.

The two friends continued along the road, Mr Dog wanting to put a safe distance between himself and the farmer. Hog lay draped over Mr Dog's back, snoring now and then as he snoozed. The clouds were starting to darken in the late-afternoon sky when the sound of another engine thrummed through the landscape. A car was coming!

Mr Dog quickly hid among the long grass and buttercups at the side of the road, afraid it

might be the farmer. But no, this was a red Land
Rover driven by an old woman, towing a trailer
loaded with chopped-up logs for firewood. As
the Land Rover rattled past, Mr Dog waited,
poised to spring.

'Hold on tight,' he told Hog. Then he ran out
and, with a majestic leap, landed in the trailer on
the logs.

'WHEEE!' cried Hog through a

mouthful of neckerchief as he clung to Mr Dog's

back. 'That was an amazing jump.'

'I believe I was a racehorse in a former life,'

said Mr Dog with a chuckle. 'Now we can travel

further, faster – and in style!'

The road wound along through fields and moors, and Mr Dog watched them go by, quietly regaining his strength. But as the trailer turned left at a junction and trundled past a stretch of woodland, he caught a sudden sniff of danger.

Hog stiffened beside him, nose twitching too. 'I recognise that smell . . .'

Ahead of them, Dandy the basset was pushing out from the forest edge. Just behind him came three more dogs – a harrier, a bloodhound and a ridgeback.

'It's the hounds from last night!' Mr Dog flattened himself down over the logs in the trailer. 'They said I'd regret picking your side . . .'

Hog was shaking. 'You mean they're roaming free, and looking for us?'

Dandy sniffed the air – then turned sharply towards the trailer. His floppy ears practically stood on end as he saw Mr Dog.

'They're not looking for us, Hog,' said Mr Dog grimly. 'I'm afraid they've *found* us!'

'There he is!' Dandy howled. 'I can smell that hedgehog too. After them!'

The hounds came charging after the trailer, barking and yapping. Mr Dog saw the fury in Dandy's face. *I normally get on terribly well with bassets*, he reflected. *It just goes to show: there are no mean dog breeds – only mean dogs.*

'We're going too fast for them,' Hog realised as the car accelerated away. The angry hounds grew smaller and smaller, until they were lost from view round the next corner. 'They can't catch up! Yay!'

'What a relief,' Mr Dog agreed – just as the old lady's car began to slow down again. 'Oh, no!' Up ahead he could see that some cattle were being led from one field to another. They were completely blocking the road. 'We'll be stuck here for ages.'

'That means that Dandy and the others will catch up with us.' Hog had already curled into a ball. 'Oh, no. Oh, EEEP! They're going to get us!'

Chapter Eight

INTO THE WOODS

As the old lady's car slowed down further, Mr Dog made a quick decision. 'I've enjoyed the ride, but I think this is our stop. Come on, Hog!' Mr Dog snatched up Hog and made an enormous leap from the still-moving trailer, clear over the top of a big clump of nettles. Hitting the ground running, he disappeared into the woods.

'But they're sniffy dogs, Mr Dog!' Hog squeaked. 'Won't they just follow your trail?'

'My scent will be stronger in the trailer,' Mr Dog panted. 'I jumped the bush so I wouldn't leave an obvious track. Hopefully by the time they realise we're not hiding in the old lady's log pile, we'll have a good head start!'

The four hounds came yapping and barking round the corner. The trailer had stopped moving by now, and Dandy put on a burst of speed on his sturdy little legs, eager to catch up. But the cattle saw the dogs running at them and started to mill about in alarm, mooing. The

farmer frowned and shouted a warning at the dogs. The harrier and the bloodhound held back, but Dandy and the ridgeback jumped on to the trailer, sniffing about furiously. The old woman got out of her car and started waving her arms at them, shooing them out.

'So far, so good,' said Mr Dog as Hog scrambled on to his back. 'But we must keep moving.'

'Where are we going?' Hog wondered, biting hard on to Mr Dog's red spotted neckerchief to hold on.

'For now, anywhere that Dandy and his friends are not,' said Mr Dog. 'It's the only way to keep you safe.'

The pair set off again. Mr Dog's legs ached, but he didn't dare stop. He knew the hounds would be able to pick up even a faint trail, given enough time. To his relief, he chanced upon a stream running through the wood and drank thirstily.

'We must travel on through the water,' he said. 'That way, we'll leave no trail or scent at all.'

'Clever!' Hog jumped into the stream and started paddling away. 'You need a rest from carrying me. I'll swim alongside you.'

Mr Dog gave him a grin and splashed into the water after him. 'Nothing like an afternoon swim when you're all hot and dusty, eh?'

They set off through the stream, but Mr Dog's

good mood didn't last long. He could already hear the yap of Dandy and the hounds in the distance.

The day was turning to dusk, and Hog began to tire. Mr Dog lifted him up, dripping, from the water and jumped out on to the bank, being careful to leave no tracks.

'Where are we going to go, Mr Dog?' asked Hog. 'Where can a little hedgie like me find safety?'

'We'll find somewhere,' Mr Dog told him. 'What we need is someone local . . . someone who knows the area . . .'

'You called, pets?' came a high, wavery voice from behind them. 'If it's safety for hedgies you're after, I may be able to help!'

The voice seemed to belong to the stump of a tree. Mr Dog gently dropped Hog as another hedgehog popped up. It was a very plump and elderly hedgehog, her prickles grey but her eyes bright with wisdom.

'How do you do,' said Mr Dog politely. 'I'm Mr
Dog and this is Hog. And what is your name, may
I ask?'

'I'm Maura,' said the old hedgie. 'I am forty
seasons old.' She smiled proudly. 'In hedgehog

years, that's about one hundred and four!'

Mr Dog's jaw dropped. 'To have lived for so long, you must know all the best places for a hedgie to hide!'

'Not only that, pet. I happen to be very well bred.' Maura raised her little twitchy nose up in the air. 'I am descended from the very first hedgehogs on the Isle of Evan.'

'The very first?' Hog marvelled. 'How do you know?'

'Because the very first hedgehogs on this island were brought across from the mainland over a thousand seasons ago,' Maura explained. 'The lady who owns these lands wanted hedgies

to eat the slugs and snails in her garden. Well,

they did, of course, as hedgies do. And in time,

they had little hoglets, and those hoglets grew up

and *they* had hoglets . . .'

Mr Dog nodded. 'So the hedgehog population grew and grew.'

Hog was fidgeting. 'Um, please, Mr Dog, shouldn't we be finding that place to hide?'

'Soon, Hog. I think we're learning the reason why hedgehogs have to hide at all.' Mr Dog turned back to Maura and grinned. 'The D-O-G in my surname is short for "DO-Go on"...!'

'Thank you, pet. I shall.' Maura seemed pleased. 'With quiet roads, no predators and a huge amount of delicious wader eggs nearby, it was a hedgie paradise. My ancestors were the first to be brought here, yes, but soon there were

thousands of hedgies on the Isle of Evan.'

'And that must have affected the other wildlife,' Mr Dog realised.

'Like the wader birds!' Hog wheezed in alarm. 'It's like you said, Mr Dog. The birds were always able to hatch their eggs here safely until us hedgies came along and started to eat them . . .'

Mr Dog nodded sadly. 'I hate to say it, but it sounds as if Mrs Maitland was right – hedgehogs *don't* belong on the Isle of Evan.'

Maura bristled. 'It's not my family's fault we were kidnapped and set to work here, is it?'

'It's not any hedgehog's fault,' Hog agreed.

'No, it isn't,' said Mr Dog. 'Which is why

Lizzie Toddy "Busybody" is trying to deal with the situation kindly, even while Mrs Maitland and her friends are hunting you down.'

'Lizzie Toddy, you say?' Maura nodded. 'Why, these woods back on to her garden, pet. Her farm is the safe place I was going to tell you about!'

'Marvellous,' woofed Mr Dog. 'Which way do we go? I'm all ears!' And he shook his shaggy ears about to prove it. As he did so, he heard distant snorting and yapping from somewhere in the woods.

'You'd better tell us fast, Maura,' said Hog. 'Some hounds are coming. They must've picked up our scent.'

'You'll be in danger too, Maura,' Mr Dog realised.

'In my younger days, I could climb this tree,' Maura said wistfully. 'Hedgies are quite the climbers, you know! But as it is, I'll just curl up.' She demonstrated, revealing her hundreds of extra-spiky prickles. 'No dog's silly enough to bother me! Tatty-bye, pets!'

'Wait! Which way do we go?' Mr Dog pawed the ground in front of her. 'You haven't told us yet!'

'No time!' Hog cried, beetling away towards the cover of a nearby bush. 'Run for it, Mr Dog!' But as he vanished under the leaves, there came a

clang of metal and a frightened 'Eeep!'

Mr Dog dashed over and bit at the bush's branches. They came away easily to reveal an old rusted cage of wire mesh beneath. 'A vermin trap!' he breathed. Some of the bars were bent, leaving a gap – not quite enough to let a hedgie get out, but enough for determined paws to get in.

'I can't leave you here, Hog,' said Mr Dog.

'Dandy and his friends might get you.'

Hog was shivering with fear. 'But if you stay,

they'll get us both for sure!'

Chapter Nine

ATTACK FROM ABOVE!

Mr Dog had come across traps like this before.

The cage door had closed as Hog blundered inside and brushed against the catch. Now it was jammed tight and, though he bit at the

rusty bars and pulled with all his strength, he couldn't budge it.

The sound of the hounds crashing through the undergrowth was getting louder.

'I'll try to lead them away,' Mr Dog told Hog, nudging the branches back over the cage. 'Hopefully they'll chase after me and lose your scent. I'll circle round and get back to you just as soon as I can.'

Hog was rocking from side to side. 'But what if they catch you?'

'I'm quick on my paws,' Mr Dog assured him. But then he heard the sound of something bigger and larger thumping through the woods.

'What's this?' A woman with blonde frizzy hair, red gardening gloves and a red coat came running into sight. 'I thought I heard woofing and the scream of a frightened hedgie . . .' She scowled at Mr Dog. 'Get away from that cage! Go on, shoo!'

Me? thought Mr Dog indignantly.

Lizzie pulled the cage from under the bush. 'My old trap caught the hedgie before you could hurt him, thank goodness.' She looked up at the sound of Dandy and his pack-mates crashing through the bracken, then back at Mr Dog. 'You can't have this hedgie. Go on, get back to your friends.'

'They're no friends of mine, madam!' Mr Dog protested, but of course to her it only sounded like woofing, and seemed to make her crosser. She lifted the cage to head height out of any animal's reach, wedged it in the fork of two sturdy branches in Maura's tree and opened the door, ready to scoop Hog out from inside.

'Get off me!' squealed Hog, wriggling away from her fingers. 'Help!'

'She won't hurt you, Hog,' barked Mr Dog. 'This is Lizzie, she wants to help . . .'

Lizzie looked again at Mr Dog. 'Wait a moment. Hey, didn't I see you at the harbour yesterday? Are you the stray dog that Moaning Minnie Maitland's been on about?'

Mr Dog quickly sat down and offered a paw as a show of friendship.

She looked at him thoughtfully. 'You don't seem very wild and dangerous to me . . .'

'But those hounds are!' Hog was looking through the bars of his cage and trembling. 'Run,

Mr Dog! The sniffy dogs are coming!'

The next moment, Dandy came thundering through the undergrowth, barking ferociously. Mr Dog reared up in alarm, and the ridgeback came flying at him and knocked him over backwards. Mr Dog quickly rolled and got back to his paws – only for the bloodhound and the harrier to hare up and knock him down again. Mr Dog fell, winded, barking in warning, but the other dogs yapped louder.

'No!' Lizzie said sternly – leaving Hog in the cage up in the tree, she quickly jumped between Mr Dog and the hounds. 'Four against one isn't fair, is it? Where are your owners? Get off with you.'

But the hounds did not back down. 'She can't

keep you safe from us,' Dandy yapped. 'Nobody

can!'

But Mr Dog wasn't looking at the blustering

basset any more. His eyes were fixed on Hog,

who'd now crept out of the cage . . . and, perhaps

inspired by Maura's talk of climbing hedgehogs,

was starting to wriggle up the tree branch!

Lizzie hadn't noticed her prickly escaping

prisoner, trying to keep eye contact with Dandy,

the leader of the pack. 'You're as stubborn as

your owner, aren't you? And almost as annoying!'

At first, Mr Dog thought that Hog was just scared and trying to escape. Then he realised that Hog was in fact bravely balancing on the branch right above the threatening hounds, even while Lizzie tried to calm them down . . .

'No, Hog!' Mr Dog woofed.

But he was too late. Suddenly, Hog jumped!

'GERONIMOOOO!'

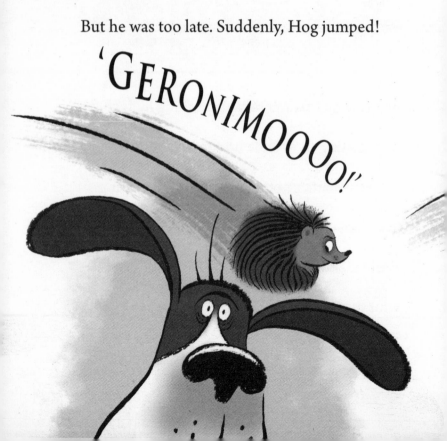

Curling into a ball, Hog landed on Dandy's head, his prickles poking between the basset's floppy ears. Dandy yelped and jumped in surprise, as Hog bounced off – and biffed the barking bloodhound on the bonce too. As he rebounded, Hog hit the harrier's head as well! With perfect timing, Mr Dog dashed forward, barged the ridgeback aside and caught Hog neatly in his jaws like a spiky ball.

Then he retreated behind Lizzie. He needn't have worried, though. Yelping in surprise and confusion, the hounds had hightailed it away, with Dandy fleeing after them through the woods.

'Not so scary after all, were they?' said Hog happily.

'Dandy's bark was worse than his bite, as we dogs say.' Mr Dog put the hedgie down and gave his nose a fond nuzzle. 'You were amazing, Hog! You stopped that situation before it could get nasty.'

'You've helped me so much,' said Hog. 'I wanted to help you too.'

Lizzie was staring down at Mr Dog and Hog in wonder. 'You two are quite the double act, aren't you?'

Mr Dog sat politely and, again, offered a paw.

'I have the strangest feeling that you were trying to help this little guy all along, not hurt him. Which makes you all right with me.' Lizzie bent down and carefully picked up Hog. 'I'm going to take you home and put you in a nice cosy carry-case. I'll look after you until I've caught enough hedgies to take back to the mainland again, and then you'll start a safer, happier life . . .'

Mr Dog lay down on his side

and gave a happy sigh. 'That IS good news.'

'But what about all the other poor hedgehogs?' said Maura, popping up again from the leaves. 'For every one that Lizzie saves, Moaning Minnie Maitland deals with two more. It's not fair!'

No, it's not, thought Mr Dog. *But whatever can be done about it now?*

Chapter Ten

A NEW START

Mr Dog followed Lizzie back to her farmhouse. It turned out that she fed her rescued hedgies dog food, and plenty of it! She put out bowls for both her new guests in one of the outbuildings.

'Delicious!' Hog declared, munching on kibble

inside his nice, cosy carry-case.

'I'm glad to hear it.' Mr Dog licked his chops
as he finished his own meal. 'Better than wader
eggs?'

Hog licked his little food dish. 'A hundred
times better, I bet!'

'I agree,' came a little squeak from behind him.

'Me too,' came another.

'I recognise those voices,' Hog gasped. 'Sprackle! Tucker! My little hedgie friends!'

'Really?' Mr Dog gave his biggest doggy grin and stood on his back legs to greet the little hedgehogs, each in a pet crate. 'Hog was afraid he'd lost you.'

'It was a human giant called Jed who found us,' said Sprackle. 'He said we would be checked to be sure we're healthy, then taken to a place called Mainland to begin a better life.'

'Mainland,' Hog said dreamily. 'That's where the first hedgehogs came from, a thousand seasons past.'

'Wow!' Tucker was impressed. 'You sure know a lot, Hog.'

'Jed the giant was waiting for his friend, frizzy Lizzie, to come back,' Sprackle said. 'He hoped she'd be bringing good news. Is finding Hog the good news?'

'It's the best news,' said Mr Dog. 'But I suppose Jed must've meant something else.'

'I wonder what?' said Hog.

Then the farmhouse doorbell rang.

Mr Dog trotted back to the house to see who was calling – and as Lizzie and Jed opened the door, he found it wasn't good news at all. Mrs Maitland had come to call, and she didn't look

pleased. Dandy, back on his lead, growled crossly.

'That no-good stray!' Mrs Maitland pointed at Mr Dog. 'What's he doing here?'

'He's staying with me for a while, until I take him back to the mainland,' said Lizzie. 'Like my hedgies, he can start another life there.'

I'm rather fond of the one I have, thought Mr Dog. *But you're very sweet to think of me!*

'That dog's been out worrying sheep,' said Mrs Maitland. 'Ought to be locked up.'

Jed folded his arms. 'What about your Dandy? I heard Farmer Donaldson say he gave a whole herd of cattle a fright, running off the lead with his friends.'

119

'They gave me a scare too,' Lizzie added. 'Still,
I do hope that all those hounds have been safely
recovered?'

'Yes.' Mrs Maitland harrumphed. 'I was out
all day searching for Dandy. Found him and the
others skulking in the woods near here and got
them all in my van. Something had spooked
them.'

Lizzie winked at Mr Dog.
'I can't imagine what.'

Mr Dog grinned.
'Beware of low-flying
hedgies,' he woofed,
and Dandy cringed.

Mrs Maitland stepped up to Lizzie. 'I'm here because I believe that you and Jed turned that stray dog loose on purpose to sabotage our hunt,' she went on. 'What do you say to that, hmm?'

'It's not true,' Lizzie said.

Jed nodded. 'We would never do such a thing, because the poor thing could've been hurt – just like those hedgehogs you find.'

Lizzie smiled. 'Still, the good news is, the Isle of Evan's hedgehogs are finally safe from your horrible hunts, Mrs Maitland. Because, you see, I didn't just go to the mainland to release our rescued hedgies. I invited members of the Scottish Nature Trust along, to see what we're doing.'

'Aye, she did,' said Jed, waving a piece of paper. 'And they were so impressed, they've just confirmed that they're banning all hedgehog hunts on the Isle of Evan. They want to help fund our "catch-with-kindness" scheme instead.'

Mrs Maitland had gone very pale. '*Ban?*' she spluttered. 'Fund *you?*'

'Hurray!' Mr Dog threw back his head and howled with happiness.

Dandy dropped to the floor, whining. 'Not fair!'

'It's good news for sure,' Mr Dog agreed. 'And, goodbye!' He scampered away to tell Hog and the other hedgies. They couldn't believe their little ears!

'No more hunts?' said Hog, his black eyes wide with wonder. 'A new start for all of us?'

'Well, I don't suppose it's possible to move *all* of the hedgehogs here back to the mainland,' said Mr Dog. 'But hopefully they can find the right balance so that the island's wildlife will live together in harmony. I can't wait to slip out and share the news with Maura!'

'How kind you are,' said Hog happily. 'Will you come back after, Mr Dog?'

'Of course, for a while,' he wuffed. 'We'll all take the ferryboat back to the mainland and I can see you settled into your new lives before carrying on my way.'

'Thank you.' Hog pressed his little nose through the bars in his carry-case and Mr Dog pushed his big nose up against it. 'I never would have got here without you.'

'Well, I couldn't leave you behind, could I?' Mr Dog grinned. 'After all, it's not every day that I meet a talking hedge . . . and practically *never* that I meet a hedge called Hog!'

Notes from the Author

There's something special and different about hedgehogs. With their sharp, prickly coats, beady eyes and little snouts they might not look that beautiful – and they are very shy – but there is nothing like them anywhere else in Britain. I love watching the way they snuffle for food or curl into a ball if they think they are in danger. And I still wait up at night sometimes, watching very quietly, hoping one will appear in my London garden (even though it never has!).

Hedgehogs live in both the town and the country and really don't usually need much more than the right food and somewhere dark and quiet to hide. But sometimes in this busy human world this isn't easy, so occasionally we just have to give them a bit of help. Remember that one might be living in a pile of dead leaves or under a bush or compost heap, so be careful if you disturb them. If you have a hedgehog nearby, think about whether you might leave out a little extra food when it's time for them to get ready to hibernate for the winter or when they have just woken up in the spring. They will happily eat dog food or cat food and like water (not milk) to drink. And if anyone is lighting a bonfire, ask them to check for hedgehogs first!

Hedgehogs are nocturnal animals so they only usually go out at night. If you see one during the day, it might have a problem. If you find a hedgehog in daylight and it looks lost, don't touch it but ring your local hedgehog rescue centre or a hedgehog charity instead for advice. Hedgehogs really need our friendship – even if they can't tell us so.

Read on for a sneak peek of
Mr Dog's next adventure,

MR DOG

AND THE FARAWAY FOX

Chapter One

A CRY IN THE NIGHT

It was late in the city. The roads were quiet and the house windows were dark. But not all animals went to bed just because humans did! Nocturnal creatures still roamed the streets and gardens ...

An eerie sound, like a howling scream, rose up into the starry springtime blackness of the sky.

Mr Dog jumped awake, his dark eyes wide

under their bushy brows. He was a raggedy mutt, with dark scruffy fur, a big black nose and front paws as white as his muzzle. 'What a curious noise,' he said to himself, stretching with a yawn. 'I wonder what it was?'

The short, sad, yowling cry came again. Mr Dog pit-patted across the kitchen to the back door, stuck his head out through the cat flap and raised an ear. He was trying to trace the lonely sound. But the night was quiet again, just the grumble of a passing car in a nearby road, so he went back inside.

Mr Dog didn't often stay in cities. A travelling dog by nature, he preferred fresh air, fields and forests. If he chose to stay with a pet owner it was usually in a sleepy town or small-time village. But a little while ago he had stepped on a thorn and his paw had grown sore. He'd limped into town in search of help.

Luckily, a kind, animal-loving lady called Minnah had found him and taken him home. She'd pulled out the thorn with tweezers, given him a good bath and even washed the red-and-white spotted hanky that served as his collar! Her friend was a vet who had checked Mr Dog's paw, and luckily the only treatment needed was to soak it in a special bath for ten minutes, twice a day.

'It's really feeling much better already,' thought Mr Dog, waggling his paw. 'And how sweet and clean I smell! I may have to change my name to Lord Dog…' He stood on his back paws and tried to look as posh as possible. 'Hmm, perhaps even *Sir* Dog?'

'Sir Silly Dog!' someone giggled from a pet-carrier on the kitchen floor.

'Silly? I'm being serious.' Mr Dog beamed at the tortoise inside the carrier. 'Or *sir*-ious, at least.

How are you feeling, Shelly?'

Shelly pushed out his little scaly head. 'I'm feeling glad to have such a noble neighbour!' he said. Shelly was a fifteen-year-old Horsfield tortoise with a richly patterned shell and a sense of fun that was missing in many tortoises. 'I just really hope that someone finds poor old Crawly soon.'

'So do I,' Mr Dog agreed sadly. Crawly was another tortoise who for years had lived with Shelly in a nearby garden. Then, two days ago, Crawly had gone missing. There was no sign of forced entry to the garden. No one knew what had happened. Since the tortoises' owners had to go away for a few days, they'd asked Minnah to look after Crawly in case something happened to him too.

'One minute Crawly was there beneath a

hedge,' Shelly said, not for the first time, 'and the next minute . . . he was gone.' Shelly's head slowly shrank back inside his shell. 'It all happened so fast.'

'Don't lose hope.' Mr Dog put his nose to the side of the carry-case and snuffled Shelly's shell. 'Crawly might still show up, you know . . .' Suddenly he heard the creak of a floorboard. The kitchen light flicked on and Minnah came into the room.

'Hello, boy,' she yawned, patting his head. Mr Dog woofed softly in greeting and wagged his brushy tail.

'That screaming fox woke you up too, did it?' said Minnah, filling the kettle. 'What a racket, calling out like that . . .'

'A fox!' Shelly shivered in his shell – though, of course, Minnah couldn't hear a word he said.

'I never knew that a fox could make a sound like that.'

'Nor me,' Mr Dog agreed. 'Minnah certainly taught us something tonight.'

Shelly's dark eyes twinkled. 'You mean . . . she "*tortoise*" something!'

Mr Dog rolled on to his back and wriggled in amusement. Shelly beamed.

Minnah made herself a cup of tea, fed Mr Dog a biscuit and then switched out the light and went back up to bed.

Mr Dog had just settled himself back in his basket when the eerie fox cry sounded again.

'I don't like the thought of a fox being so close by,' Shelly confessed. 'My owner said it could've been a fox who took Crawly from the garden.'

'I hope not,' said Mr Dog, who was a friend to all animals and never one to judge. 'Dogs and foxes tend to avoid each other, so I haven't really met one before . . .'

After a while, Shelly fell asleep. But Mr Dog's ears jumped as the strange howl sounded once more from outside.

I wonder why that fox is calling? thought Mr Dog. *Perhaps it's in trouble. Maybe I can help?* Limping just a little, Mr Dog padded over to the catflap and squeezed through it. *At the very least, I can ask him to keep the noise down so he doesn't disturb the neighbours . . .*

The catflap opened on to a side alley: one way led to the main street, the other to a quiet lane that backed on to a row of garages. The night was cool and Mr Dog's nose twitched with the city's scents. The houses were dark but the streetlamps cast bright orange patches over the pavements. Somewhere distant, gulls gave their rowdy cries and a clock struck three. Mr Dog felt happy. How nice it was to be outside again!

His nose twitched with a strong, musky smell from the fir trees that lined someone's garden. *That fox has marked this territory*, thought Mr Dog. *A boy fox, unless I'm very much mistaken. He must be close by . . .*

Then Mr Dog caught another smell.

The smell of a tortoise!

Quickly he pushed his head through the fir trees – and couldn't believe his eyes.

A small and scrappy red fox was sitting happily in the garden – holding a tortoise in its jaws!